JellyTelly Press is a division of JellyTelly, LLC.

FaithWords is a division of Hachette Book Group, Inc. The FaithWords name and logo are trademarks of Hachette Book Group, Inc.

FaithWords
Hachette Book Group
1290 Avenue of the Americas, New York, NY 10104

hachettebookgroup.com | faithwords.com | jellytelly.com

Buck Denver and Friends created by Phil Vischer. Buck Denver Asks®.. What's in the Bible? trademark and character rights are owned by Phil Vischer IP, LLC and used by permission under license from Jellyfish One, LLC.

Written by Phil Vischer
Illustrated by Greg Hardin and Kenny Yamada

Art Direction and Design: John Trent
Creative Direction: Phil Vischer and Anne Fogerty

First Edition: February 2019

Scripture quotations are from the ESV® Bible (The Holy Bible, English Standard Version®), copyright © 2001 by Crossway, a publishing ministry of Good News Publishers. Used by permission. All rights reserved.

Library of Congress Cataloging-in-Publication Data has been applied for.
10 9 8 7 6 5 4 3 2 1
ISBN: 978-1-5460-1187-3
Printed in China
APS

Buck Denver's
GIANT
Robot Suit
A Lesson in FRIENDSHIP

Written by Phil Vischer
Illustrated by Greg Hardin & Kenny Yamada

Sunday School Lady and Marcy jumped.

"What was THAT?" Marcy asked. "It made me spill my glue!"

Sunday School Lady and Marcy were getting crafts ready for kids' church on Sunday.

The loud CRASH outside had scared them and sent glue flying on to the floor, the wall, and even the ceiling!

"Let's see what happened!" said Sunday School Lady. "Then we'll come back and clean up this mess."

"Whoa," said Marcy as they stepped outside the church.

"It's a giant robot!"

It DID look like a giant robot.

A BROKEN giant robot in a pile of garbage cans.

A broken giant robot in a pile of garbage cans with Buck Denver in the middle!

"Buck! Are you okay?" Sunday School Lady asked as she ran over to help.

"I think so," said Buck. He was a little dizzy. Marcy helped him up.

"Why do you want to be a giant robot?" Marcy asked.

"Why WOULDN'T I?" Buck answered. "These robot arms make me stronger so I can help more people. And these robot legs make me so tall I feel like I'm closer to God! I can almost see Him!"

Sunday School Lady thought for a minute.

"Buck, what if I told you there was an easier way to be stronger AND closer to God?" Sunday School Lady asked.

Buck thought. "Easier than turning yourself into a giant robot?"

"MUCH easier than turning yourself into a giant robot!" Sunday School Lady replied.

Buck thought harder. "I'd say that would be pretty great. What's your secret? Magic beans? Special vitamins? A new app for my phone?"

"No." Sunday School Lady smiled. "**FRIENDSHIP.**"

Buck was confused. "FRIENDSHIP is like a giant robot suit?"

"You wanted robot arms to make you stronger. I know a boy who became stronger because of FRIENDSHIP. Should we visit him?" Sunday School Lady asked.

"Sure!" Buck replied.

"The boy I'm thinking of lived about 3,000 years ago!" Sunday School Lady said, pulling out her trusty flannelgraph.

"Then how can we visit him?" Buck asked.

Sunday School Lady smiled. "Because this isn't an ordinary flannelgraph. It's a MAGIC flannelgraph!"

Buck looked worried. "Wait—is this going to hurt?"

"Not as much as crashing into the garbage in a robot suit!" said Marcy.

"Magic Flannelgraph ... take us to DAVID!"
Sunday School Lady tapped her pointer and BOOM!

Suddenly Buck wasn't looking at the flannelgraph,
he was IN the flannelgraph!

"**AAAH!**" Buck yelled.
"I feel fuzzy!"

Marcy laughed. "That's because it's flannel!
You'll get used to it."

"You've heard of King David, right, Buck?"
asked Sunday School Lady.

Buck nodded. "Sure I have. He was Israel's best king!
He was super strong and super brave!"

"Isn't he the guy that fought Goliath? The giant?" Marcy asked.

"He was!" Sunday School Lady answered. "That took courage!
But AFTER that, things got rough for David!"

"David was just a boy when he beat Goliath, which made him really popular. SO popular that King Saul, the first king of Israel, started to get angry.

King Saul thought David was getting TOO popular. Maybe even more popular than himself!"

"Since King Saul wanted to be the most popular guy in Israel, he started to hate David. He even wanted to KILL David!"

"That's terrible!" Buck yelled. "David was trying to help him!"

"Yes, he was," said Sunday School Lady. "But King Saul was so jealous he didn't care. He wanted David GONE."

"But God helped David. God gave David a best friend. His best friend's name was Jonathan. Jonathan was ALSO King Saul's son!"

"Wait!" Buck was amazed. "David's best friend is the son of the guy who wants to KILL him?"

Sunday School Lady smiled. "I know! It's crazy, but it's true! Jonathan found out that King Saul had a plan to kill David, so he ran and told David so he could get away!"

"Jonathan helped David stay alive—not just once, but many times! Jonathan shared his robe and sword with David. He helped David grow stronger. With Jonathan's help, David became a great leader and soldier. When it was his turn to be king, David became the best king Israel ever had!"

"Wow!" Buck yelled. "Friends can make us stronger!"

"That's right, Buck," said Sunday School Lady. "God uses friends to help us in lots of ways. God had big plans for David, and he used David's friend Jonathan to help!"

Buck Denver thought about the story.

"If friends can make me stronger, I guess I don't need a robot suit for that. But what if I want to be closer to God? Is there a friend who can help me with that?"

Sunday School Lady smiled even bigger. "Pastor Paul?"

And BOOM! There was Pastor Paul inside the flannelgraph!

"Mmm ... fuzzy!" he said.
"Like my favorite teddy bear, Poopsie!"

Buck stared. "You have a teddy bear named 'Poopsie?'"

"Oh, yes," said Pastor Paul. "I've had him since I was small. We've been friends forever!"

"Speaking of which," Marcy chimed in. "Tell us about this friend who can get us closer to God!"

"We need to take a little trip! Follow me!"
Pastor Paul yelled excitedly.

Suddenly they were in a room where a group of men sat around a table. They were eating a meal and listening to one man in the middle.

"That's Jesus!" Buck yelled.

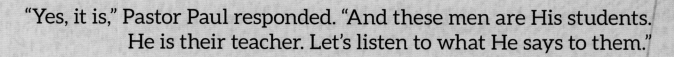

"Yes, it is," Pastor Paul responded. "And these men are His students. He is their teacher. Let's listen to what He says to them."

As they listened, Jesus said ...

"No longer do I call you servants, for the servant does not know what his master is doing; but I have called you friends, for all that I have heard from my Father I have made known to you."

Buck smiled. "Jesus calls them His friends. He's not just their teacher—He's their friend!"

"That's nice and all," Marcy said. "But how does that get them closer to God?"

Pastor Paul smiled big. "Because Jesus IS God! Jesus shows us God—and lets us get close to God—because He IS God!"

Buck Denver was amazed.

"Whoa," he whispered. "Jesus wants to be more than my teacher. He wants to be my friend. And being close to Jesus brings us close to God, because Jesus IS God!"

"You got it, Buck!" Sunday School Lady said. She tapped the ground with her pointer one more time ...

... and suddenly everyone was back at the church.

"So what did we learn about friendship?" Sunday School Lady asked.

"God uses friends to help us grow stronger, like David and Jonathan!" Buck said.

"But best of all," he continued, "being friends with Jesus brings us closer to God! When we become friends with Jesus, we become friends with God!"

"You really learned a lot today, Buck!"
Sunday School Lady said happily.

"I sure did!" Buck answered. "Next, I need to learn
what to do with a used robot suit."

Marcy thought for a moment. "I think I have an idea ... "

"What do you know?" said Buck. "Robot suits might not be good at getting us closer to God, but they're REALLY good at cleaning glue off the ceiling!"

Family Connection

Help your family **KNOW** the love of God,
GROW in God's love, and **SHOW** God's love to others.

CONNECT after reading:

ASK:

1. Why was Buck wearing a giant robot suit?
2. What makes a good friend? Think about a time you needed a friend. Who was there for you? What did they do?
3. How was Jonathan a good friend to David?
4. Why do you think it's important to know that Jesus calls us His friends?

READ:

- Read more about David and Jonathan's friendship in **1 Samuel 18:1-5**.
- Learn what Jesus said to His disciples about friendship in **John 15:12-17**.

REMEMBER:

God uses friends to help us grow stronger and our friendship with Jesus brings us closer to God!

"This is my commandment, that you love one another as I have loved you."
John 15:12

Take turns praying and thanking God for your friends and for His friendship!

For more family fun, check out jellytelly.com, a partner for Christian parents.